SAY "AHHH!"

Dora Goes to the Doctor

by Phoebe Beinstein
illustrated by A&J Studios

SIMON AND SCHUSTER/NICKELODEON

Based on the TV series *Dora the Explorer* as seen on Nick Jr.

SIMON AND SCHUSTER
First published in Great Britain in 2009 by Simon & Schuster UK Ltd
1st Floor, 222 Gray's Inn Road, London WC1X 8HB
A CBS Company

Originally published in the USA in 2008 by Simon Spotlight,
an imprint of Simon & Schuster Children's Division, New York.

A CIP catalogue record for this book is available from the British Library

ISBN: 978-0-85707-419-5
Printed in China

10 9 8 7 6 5 4 3

Visit our websites: www.simonandschuster.co.uk
                    www.nick.co.uk

¡Hola! *Soy* Dora. Today my *mami* is taking me for a checkup at the doctor's. Will you come with me? Great! *¡Vámonos!*

First we have to find the examination room. Then the doctor will give me my checkup. Who do we ask for help when we don't know which way to go? Yeah, Map!

Map says first we have to go to the bus stop to catch the number four bus which will take us to the doctor's surgery. Then we go into the waiting room where the nurse will call us into the examination room for my checkup.

Here we are at the bus stop. There are three buses coming. Can you see the number four bus? That's the one that will take us to the doctor's surgery.

There it is! *¡Número cuatro!* Number four! *¡Vámonos!* Let's get on the bus!

The bus took us to the doctor's surgery, but the door to the waiting room is closed. The sign says press the buzzer. Will you help me press the buzzer? Press it! *Buzz! Buzz!*

Nurse Pilar is opening the door to the waiting room!

Nurse Pilar says that Dr Lopez will be ready for us in a few minutes. There are lots of books and toys in the waiting room. Look at the puzzle on the floor! It's a picture of the human body. The heart is missing. Will you help me find it? *¡Gracias!*

Mami said that Nurse Pilar just called my name. That means we can go into the examination room for my checkup!

The first thing Nurse Pilar does is weigh and measure me to see how much I've grown. Wow, I've grown a lot since my last checkup. Do you know how tall you are and how much you weigh? Then she takes my temperature by putting a thermometer in my mouth. Nurse Pilar says my temperature is just right!

Now it's time for Dr Lopez to come in and examine me. First she wants to listen to my heart with her stethoscope. She even lets me listen! It goes *lub, dub, lub, dub*.
What does your heart sound like?

The next tool Dr Lopez needs is a little hammer to test my reflexes. Can you see something that looks like a little hammer?

Yes, here it is! Dr Lopez taps both my knees and makes them jump all by themselves.

Dr Lopez asks me to open my mouth wide and make an "ahhh" sound so she can look at my throat. Make an "ahhh" sound with me. Say "Ahhh!"

She takes a little stick called a tongue depressor and gently presses on my tongue so she can see my throat.

Her next tool is something called an otoscope. It has a little light on it to help her see into my eyes and ears and nose.

The last thing Dr Lopez does is feel my tummy.
She presses it a little bit all around. That tickles!
My checkup is all done. Dr Lopez used all sorts
of interesting instruments to make sure I'm healthy.
And I am healthy! *¡Tengo salud!*

Now I get to choose a toy from the toy box for being such a good patient. I can see a pink heart ring at the bottom. Will you help me reach it? Reach with your arm! Good reaching!

Mami says I was very brave at my checkup. She says you were too. I couldn't have done it without your help. *¡Gracias!*